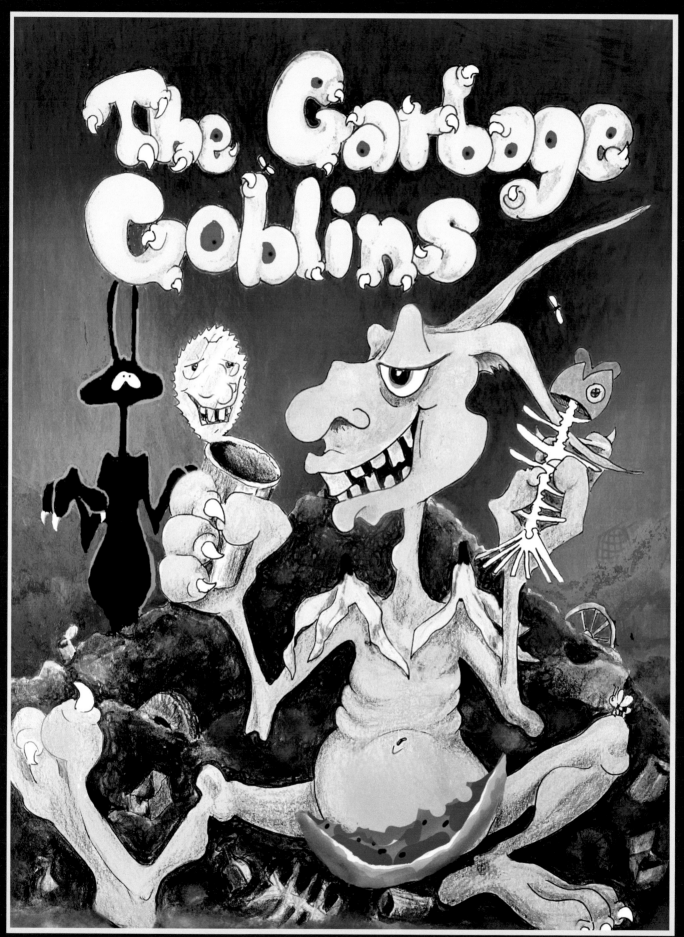

The Garbage Goblins

Walt Thorp and Linda Laird

To order additional copies of this book, contact:
Xlibris
844-714-8691
www.Xlibris.com
Orders@Xlibris.com

Interior Image Credit: Linda Laird

ISBN:	Softcover	978-1-6698-2475-6
	Hardcover	978-1-6698-2474-9
	EBook	978-1-6698-2476-3

Library of Congress Control Number: 2022908830

Print information available on the last page

Rev. date: 07/15/2022

THE
GARBAGE
GOBLINS

At a house, not far from here, on a street named Snook,
lived a boy named Bert whom the Goblins took.
With freckles of red and curly orange locks,
he's a little rascal and a chatterbox.

He loved to yell, and jump, and run,
to play and have all sorts of fun.
He was just a kid like any other,
with a father, two sisters, three cats, and a mother.

He would have been a loveable boy
if it weren't for the thing, he most enjoyed.
You see he wasn't really bad or mean,
it's just that Bert was never clean.

While other kids up and down the street
played lots of games like, Hide and Seek.
They played with toys both large and small,
like kites, and swings, and crayons and balls,
drums and things that bang and bump,
whistle or squirt, squeak, or thump.

Bert wasn't playing with the rest of his chumps.
You would find Bert playing in the dump.
The dump had so much interesting stuff.
Why being there made him feel really tough,
amid bent nails, bottles, and rusty springs,
old mattresses, cars, cans, and things,
covered with sticky goo and slippery slime,
smelly gunk and greasy grime.
To the top of the dump, he climbed.
"This is where I'll spend my time,
surrounded by junk, as far as I can see.
Why there's no place else I'd rather be!"

In the dump is where I'll stay
And day after day he'd play
all day long lost in his bliss,
never noticing anything amiss.
From dawn to dusk without rest,
he made himself a terrible mess,
with muddy knees and grimy clothes,
gritty hair, dirty ears, and a runny nose,
a brownish neck, yellow teeth,
sticky fingers and yucky feet!

He smelled so bad; you'd say he reeked.
Cats scampered and his sisters shrieked,
"Oh, Yucky, Phew, what a sight!"
when he came home that night.
His father ordered. "To the tub, Bub
and make sure you use soap to scrub!"
His mother shook her head and sighed
As she looked at his clothes she cried
"It'll take a week of scrubbing,
just to clean this ragamuffin."
"But I won't scrub, and I won't bathe,"
Bert began to rant and rave,
No, I don't like scrubs
"I hate baths and I hate suds,
I Like dirt, I won't be cleaned."
Then Burt ran off as he screamed,

"So, catch me, catch me if you can!"
Up he jumped and out the door, he ran.
He ran back to the dump with its dirt and grime,
back where he loved to spend all his time.
Back to where thirty sets of eyes,
fiery red and keen, like spies,
waited patiently, quietly watching,
and all those eyes were busy plotting.

Behind those eyes, so bright and red
were garbage goblins with giant heads.
Hiding in the trash, they took their stand.
A wicked and a horrible band,
smelly and slimy like their dumpish land,
they waited to spring their fiendish plan.

Bert wasn't afraid, he didn't look behind,
He just giggled and ran on, quite blind.
Further and further into his paradise,
a place feared by alley cats and mice.
He ran laughing amid the mountains of trash.
Then suddenly it got really, scary, really, fast.
Bert stopped suddenly and began to frown.
He looked around at the icky dark mounds,
but he never looked above his noggin.
At the top of the trash mountain, stood a goblin.

That goblin dropped a mighty snare
that snatched poor Bert up into the air.
Into a goblin's gobliny trap,
Snap, grab and that was that.
"Ha, Ha, Ha," the goblins laughed,
Knowing that they had him trapped.
They flipped poor Bert upon his back
and pulled some rope from their pack.

Then they tied his hands and feet
to a pole, quick and neat.
Then those goblins carried him off
to meet the terrible Goblin King, Groff.

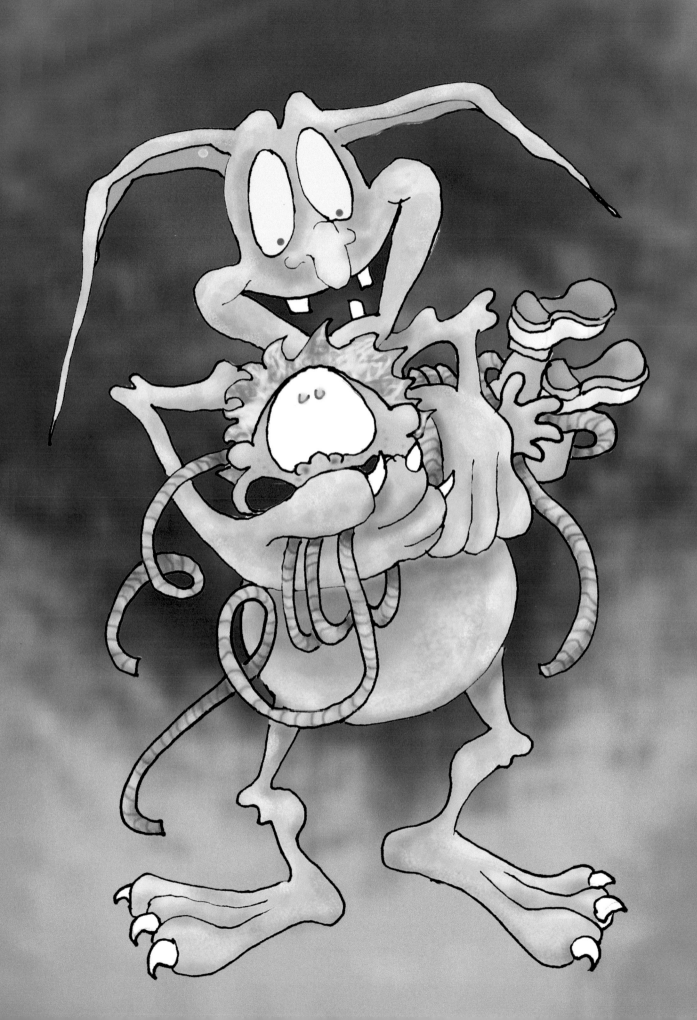

Now the goblin king was an ugly old lump
who ruled from the smelliest depths of the dump,
on a throne of sardine tins and empty jars,
in a garbage castle made of rusty cars.

Groff burped and belched, "Harrumph!"
as they dropped Bert with an awful thump.
He said, "This lad, is perfect, you see.
Why he's almost as stinky and dirty as me!
Just wait, you'll be a great goblin too,
after a dip in our goblin brewed stew."

So, huffing and puffing, that rascally pack
hauled out the stewpot, all huge and black.
And into that metal cauldron, they stuck
the snottiest, stinkiest, yuckiest stuff.
Rusty nails, banana peels, old slimy muck
and anything else, that just plain stunk,
from rotten old onions to a big black skunk.
They even threw in a smelly old bag of magic junk.

Then each of these critters grabbed a stick,
and they stirred that concoction until it was thick.
"Now," said the King, "to complete this goblin dessert,
We'll toss in the kid the humans, call Bert."
"Oh no," cried Bert, "Not me!"
"A goblin I could never be,
cause I'm not bad, evil, or mean.
It's just that I am never clean."
"Stop your whining, what's the fuss?
You're already as dirty as us."

Then thirty goblins, both large and small
began to chant and then began to call.
"Why he'll make the yuckiest goblin of all,"
said the big green goblin, who was very tall.
So, with ropes and pulleys, boards, and beams,
they hoisted poor Bert up while he screamed,
until he was inches away from the goblin pot,
just seconds away from falling, ker-plop!

There he hung while the scoundrels danced,
giggled and howled, skipped, and pranced.
Making a ruckus so great and loud,
that they finally woke up a little white cloud.
That little white cloud so fluffy and light
looked down through the night at the terrible sight.
"What do you know, "she said with a grin,
"That Groff's up to his old tricks again!
Well, I have a big, surprise for him."
And the fluffy cloud turned rather grim.

Then that tiny cloud, so soft and white
she huffed and puffed with all her might.
She got bigger, darker, and filled up the night.
She covered the sky and blocked out all light.
Then lightning flashed and thunder crashed
and the goblins begin to dart and dash.
One drop, two drops, three, four,
then it began to really pour.

It rained in sheets, showered, and stormed.
The waters rose and a river formed.
Crashing down with a deafening roar,
through the dump, the stormy river tore.
Sweeping up junk as it raced along,
and anything else that didn't belong.
It swept up the goblin's castle and slop,
And the throne with King Groff on top,
And much to the goblin's dismay
even the stewpot, was swept away
Little Bert too, was carried that day,
rolling and bouncing along in the spray.

Scrubbed clean as a washboard,
he was plunked down at his own front door.
As he stood in the doorway, he looked up and down.
He was spotlessly clean, and Bert began to frown.

Then he thought of the goblins' stew,
and their city of greasy goo.
Becoming a goblin filled him with dread,
That's when he realized he'd been misled,
He thought about his soft bed and dinner instead.
Then he thought of his parents and what they said.
That was when Bert began to see the light.
Maybe being clean was really alright!
He didn't smell like rotten mice,
in fact, he felt kind of nice.

From that day on, he brushed his teeth,
took baths and even washed his feet.
He had lots more friends now,
and that made his parents proud.
Bert was always so neat and clean,
Well, now. at least that's how it seemed...

Printed in the United States
by Baker & Taylor Publisher Services